Sal and Kim sit on the hill.
Kim has a can of pop.

But the can rolls off
and hits a rock.

A dog picks it up.
"No! The pop will fizz and fizz.
The can will go pop!"

The dog runs and runs.
The dog runs to the top
of the hill.

The can pops!
It pops on the dog!

The dog licks up
the pop!

Puzzles

Match the words that rhyme
to the pictures!

bill

kick

hill

fill

lick

lock